Clifford THE RED

CAMPING OUT

Adapted by Lisa Ann Marsoli

From the television script "Camping Out" by Scott Guy

Illustrated by Carolyn Bracken and Ken Edwards

Based on the Scholastic book series "Clifford The Big Red Dog" by Norman Bridwell

No part of this publication may be reproduced in whole or in part, or stored in a retrieval system, or transmitted in any form or by any means, electronic, mechanical, photocopying, recording, or otherwise, without written permission of the publisher. For information regarding permission, write to Scholastic Inc., Attention: Permissions Department, 557 Broadway, New York, NY 10012.

ISBN 0-439-45810-2

10 9   05 06 07

Printed in the U.S.A.
First printing, March 2003

SCHOLASTIC INC.

New York   Toronto   London   Auckland   Sydney
Mexico City   New Delhi   Hong Kong   Buenos Aires

The Howards' van rolled to a stop.

"Hooray! Let the camping trip begin!"

said Emily Elizabeth.

Everyone got out of the van quickly.

Jetta took much longer.

She had packed a lot of stuff!

"I like the comforts of home," Jetta said.

First everyone set up their tents.

Clifford had to make his out of a tree!

Mac's tent looked like a fancy doghouse.

Jetta's tent looked more like a cute cottage.

Jetta hooked up a computer inside.

"I don't want to be bored," she said.

The gang went for a hike.

Mrs. Howard heard a woodpecker.

Vaz heard a mockingbird.

Jetta wore a helmet and rode a noisy scooter.

She didn't hear a thing.

Mary found a family of raccoons.

Jetta tried to spot them as she zipped by.

Uh-oh!

"I didn't see the raccoons," Jetta complained.

"You have to stop and really look," said
Emily Elizabeth.

The friends stood by the stream.

"How will we get to the other side?"

asked Mary.

Clifford made a big red bridge across

the water.

Everyone was happy —

except for Jetta.

Soon they reached the top of the hill.

"What a great view!" said Dan.

"And so quiet," Emily Elizabeth added.

"I made it to level 20!" Jetta yelled.

Her eyes were glued to her game.

"Look! A flock of butterflies!" Charley said.

Jettta cried, "Now I'm at level 21!"

The noise scared the butterflies away.

Jetta never even saw them.

"Come on," said Mr. Howard.

"The waterfall should be just ahead."

Clifford and Emily Elizabeth led the way.

Jetta finally looked up from her game.

"Where's everybody going?" she asked.

Emily Elizabeth and Clifford spotted the

waterfall first.

They ran the rest of the way.

Clifford couldn't wait to cool off.

"Surf's up!" Emily Elizabeth yelled.

Mac dived in next. He wanted to

play with his pal Clifford.

"I'm not going into that cold water,"

said Jetta.

She took out her own heated pool!

Jetta wanted someone to join her.

But her friends liked swimming under

the waterfall. They watched frogs jump.

They giggled when fish tickled their toes.

That night, there was a cookout.

Clifford was hungry from his big day!

Jetta made TV dinners.

Then she put on a video.

Mac looked out the window and barked.

Jetta looked up at the star-filled sky.

She saw her friends enjoying the night.

"Maybe camping is more fun than

I thought," Jetta said.

She and Mac went outside.

Everyone made room.

"I was hoping you'd come join us,"

Emily Elizabeth told her.

"A shooting star!" cried Jetta. "Did you see it?"

"Yes," Emily Elizabeth said.

"But I'm even more glad *you* did!"

Do You Remember?

Circle the right answer.

1. The butterflies flew away because . . .
   a. Clifford barked at them.
   b. Charley chased them with a net.
   c. Jetta made too much noise.

2. How did the gang get across the stream?
   a. They rowed a boat.
   b. They walked over Clifford.
   c. They swam.

Which happened first?
Which happened next?
Which happened last?
Write a 1, 2, or 3 in the space after each sentence.

Clifford jumped into the water. _____

Mary spotted the raccoons. _____

Everyone put up the tents. _____

Answers: